Daryl Cobb lives in children. Daryl's writing beg jor at Virginia Commonwealth writing class inspiring and, combined with his love for music and the guitar, he discovered a passion for songwriting. This talent would motivate him for years to come and the rhythm he created with his music also found its way into the bedtime stories he later created for his children. The story "Boy on the Hill," about a boy who turns the clouds into animals, was his first bedtime story/song and was inspired by his son and an infatuation with the shapes of clouds. Through the years his son and daughter have inspired so much of his work, including "Daniel Dinosaur" and "Daddy Did I Ever Say? I Love You, Love You, Every Day."

Daryl spends a lot of his time these days visiting schools promoting literacy with his interactive educational assemblies "Teaching Through Creative Arts." These

performance programs teach children about the writing and creative process and allow Daryl to do what he feels is most important -- inspire children to read and write. He also performs at benefits and libraries with his "Music & Storytime" shows.

He is a member of the SCBWI.

Manuela Pentangelo lives in Busnago, Italy, near Milan, with her flowers, family and friends. She was born in Holland, but has lived all of her life in Italy. A student of architectural design, Manuela discovered that her dreams and goals lay elsewhere. She likes to say that she was born with a pencil in her hand, but it took a while before she realized that her path was to illustrate for children. Manuela often visits London, where she likes to sketch at the British Museum, and likes traveling to different places to find inspiration.

She is a member of the SCBWI.

Printed in the USA
10to2childrensbooks.com

Join the adventure and read!

Cobb/Pentangelo 2011

Other stories by Daryl K. Cobb and Manuela Pentangelo:

"Pirates: Do Pirates Go To School?"
"Bill the Bat Baby Sits Bella"
"Bill the Bat Finds His Way Home"
"Bill the Bat Loves Halloween"
"Barnyard Buddies:
   Perry Parrot Finds a Purpose"
"Greta's Magical Mistake"

www.darylcobb.com

"Pirates:
Legend Of the Snarlyfeet"

Written by
Daryl K. Cobb

Illustrated by
Manuela Pentagelo

10 To 2 Children's Books

ISBN 978-1456413750

Written by Daryl K. Cobb
Illustrated by Manuela Pentangelo

10 To 2 Children's Books

Time to Read

™

I dedicate this book to children everywhere because we all just want to fit in.

Daryl K. Cobb

To: Vera
Enjoy reading!
Daryl K Cobb

To my parents.

Manuela Pentangelo

When Peter woke up from his nap
he found the most intriguing map.

A note attached from Pirate Paul
said, "A most urgent pirate call."

"Join the adventure!" the caption read.
"A long and dangerous trip," it said.

"Your magic boots will bring you here,
and don't forget your pirate gear.
We will encounter many foe
so grab your boots, now go, go, go!"

Pete's pirate gear was at his side,
the captain's map at hand,
he slipped the boots onto his feet
and woke to Paul's command:

"All hands on deck!"
is what he said.
Pete knew the voice
that filled his head.

"Hoist the anchor!" yelled Captain Paul.
"Our destination is Hoganthall.
A mysterious little pirate land
with buried treasure in the sand."

"In Peter's hands,
he holds the clues,
a map that only pirates use."

"But Hoganthall," said Pirate Pete, "is home to dragons and Snarlyfeet."

"A Snarlyfeet
stands ten feet tall!"

"Breath so bad it
could blind us all!"

"They frown a lot
and never sleep!"

"Avast! Stop it," said Pirate Paul,
"I will do my best to protect you all.
Some danger we will surely find,
and ferocious foes of every kind.
A little scared you all will be
as we venture out to sea."

For seven days they sailed along
with gusting winds and pirate song.

To pass the time the crew told tales
of treasure hunts and riding whales.

A voice then echoed with delight,
"Land ho! Land ho! Land in my sight!"
In the crow's nest was first-mate Nic,
gazing through her looking stick.

Only a second or two had passed
when the ship hit land and stopped quite fast.
The crew was more than a little sore
as they picked themselves up off the floor.

"Thanks so much!" yelled Pirate Paul
to Nic dangling above them all.
"A tad more notice would be nice,
or next time you will pay the price."

"A day or two of swabbing decks,
shining boots and cleaning specks.
Ironing wrinkles from the sails
and cleaning out the garbage pails."

"Now, listen up, you scallywags,
it's time to hoist the pirate flags.
The treasure hunt is on, I'd say.
Let's talk no more, let's not delay."

"The Snarlyfeet will
know we're here so
grab your swords
and pirate gear.
Are you ready, Lad?
Today's the day!"
"Aye!" said Pete,
"I'm ready I'd say."

"Keep your eyes open," said Pirate Paul,
"this is dangerous land, if you recall."
With map in hand Pete led the hunt.
The crew all followed with Paul in front.

They moved along
at rapid speed
through a jungle
full of Jimson Weed.

They covered more
than a mile of ground,
when Peter stopped
to look around.

Startled by some rustling brush
Pete told the crew to, "Hush, hush, hush."

"Snarlyfeet," Pete heard someone say.
Their swords were drawn, the brush gave way.

Four Snarlyfeet stepped into view.
The kids stood fast, a courageous crew.

Now, Paul and Pete stood back to back
just waiting for the first attack.

Swords were drawn and the fear was high
when the Snarlyfeet began to cry.
The tears in their eyes could not be misread.
"Please, don't hurt us!" the smallest one said.

"Avast!" said Paul,
"Put your swords away.
A grave mistake was made today.
These Snarlyfeet aren't scary at all!
Not a hint of mean,
but rather quite tall.
Their breath isn't bad,
no one turned to dust.
Our fear of them was really unjust."

"We've been on our ship for nearly a week,
and a fight with you is not what we seek."
The Snarlyfeet beamed with a look of delight,
smiles so bright they could light up the night!

"We're hunting treasure," proclaimed Pirate Pete,
"a treasure that lay right under your feet!
You stand on the spot where it's buried, my friends.
That X at your feet is where this journey ends."

Legend now has it that Pirate Pete
found a king's ransom beneath Snarly's feet.

I don't know if it's true,
but I think it could be,
this tale of pirates who sailed the sea.

Pirates: The Ring of Hope

Chapter Book
for readers 10 and up

Books & Music
by Daryl Cobb

Author Visits and School Program
information at www.darylcobb.com

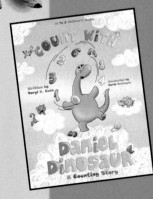

Made in the USA
Middletown, DE
11 February 2016